Anonymous

Trust in God

Three days in the life of Gellert

Anonymous

Trust in God
Three days in the life of Gellert

ISBN/EAN: 9783337367961

Printed in Europe, USA, Canada, Australia, Japan

Cover: Foto ©Andreas Hilbeck / pixelio.de

More available books at **www.hansebooks.com**

TRUST IN GOD.

TRUST IN GOD;

OR,

THREE DAYS

IN

THE LIFE OF GELLERT.

———

NEW YORK:
ROBERT CARTER AND BROTHERS
No. 530 BROADWAY.
1874.

EDWARD O. JENKINS,
Printer & Stereotyper,
No. 20 NORTH WILLIAM ST.

PREFACE.

CHRISTIAN FÜRCHTEGOTT GELLERT was born A. D. 1715, at Haynichen, in Germany, where his father was the pastor for fifty years.

After a life of many trials and great bodily infirmities, he fell asleep in the Lord on the 13th of December, A. D. 1769, aged fifty-four years. He was in his forty-eighth year at the close of the Seven Years' War

His name is famous in his native land as a writer of sacred hymns, distinguished for their simplicity, fervor,

(3)

and true devotional feeling, and which of late years have become widely known and appreciated in this country and in England, through the translations of Mrs. Winkworth and other congenial admirers.

The foundation of the following sketch is taken from the Correspondence of Gellert.

A new title is added, but the text of the original has been faithfully rendered.

May it meet with the same favor in kind, if not in degree, which it received from sympathetic minds in Germany, where a second edition of ten thousand copies has been published.

INTRODUCTION,

5

INTRODUCTION.

It was in the midst of all the horrors of the Seven Years' War, that in a little room in a house in Leipsig called the Black Post, a man might have been seen seated before his table, his head resting on his hands. He appeared sick and weak. A cotton cap covered his head, and his emaciated body was wrapped in a well-worn calico dressing-gown.

It was easy to perceive at the first glance that this closet was the study of a scholar, so many books were piled up all around him, from the enormous folio to the smaller duodecimo. There were, however, only a few on the table, and among them a Bible, which bore the marks of frequent use. It was open at the second chapter of the book of Job, and these words of the tenth verse, " What! shall we receive good at the hand of God, and shall we not receive evil?" were underscored.

This man was Christian Fürchtegott Gellert. He was reading over a hymn, with which this passage of Job, just quoted, had that moment inspired him. Gellert shared the lot of many other generous minds. It was often low tide with his revenues—never very considerable. Such was the case at this time; and to tell the truth, he did not possess a single kreutzer. The day before, however, he had possessed thirty thalers, which he had put aside to buy wood, for it was freezing hard enough to crack the very stones, and all that he had would last him but a week. As for receipts, he did not expect any. This prospect was not very pleasing to a chilly invalid. The temperature of his room seemed to realize his fears, and the window panes began to be covered with the crystal flowers, without color or perfume, which recall few cheerful thoughts to those whose windows they adorn. But when the Tempter, armed with cares, came to disturb his peace, Gellert was accustomed to meet him with another weapon, always victorious—the Sword of the Spirit, which is the word of God. He had done so at this time, and lighting on this beautiful passage in the book of Job, had meditated upon it with prayer, and under the influence of these words, had written his beautiful hymn.

" I have had my days of blessing," etc.,

a true echo of his scriptural thoughts, and of his present frame of mind.

He had just laid down his pen, and, his head resting on his hands, he said to himself, " No, I have no reason to repent of the use of those thirty thalers. Thou knowest it, O Lord, who canst read my soul! This gloom was a temptation, a want of faith! Pardon me; O Lord! I believe—help thou mine unbelief."

At this moment a knock was heard at the door, and before he could say " Come in ! " a stout little man entered, and cordially saluted Gellert. " Goodmorning, doctor," said the latter, extending his hand.

The little man seized this emaciated hand, pressed it warmly, put down his hat and cane, rubbed his hands, and cried, " Whew! how cold you are, my dear professor! This won't do! You must have more heat. Put on some wood! Such cold weather! Do you want to be really ill ? "

" My wood is out," said Gellert, sadly.

" Well, buy some more ! "

" My money is out, too," stammered Gellert, yet more embarrassed. " But —never mind—I will think of it."

The doctor, who never stopped long at one thing, then cast his eyes on the paper. " Ah!" said he, " a new hymn ? "

Gellert bowed, but he was evidently vexed. Without more ceremony, the doctor took the sheet and went to the window. " What! frosty panes, too? This is too bad!" Then, after having read it; "What fervor! What energy! What true Christian feeling! My dear sir, I must carry this off to take a copy. I will bring it back to you to-morrow. My wife, who honors you so much, must have the first sight of it You will allow me?" And without waiting for an answer, he put it in his pocket. Then approaching the professor, whose looks protested in vain against this summary proceeding, he felt his pulse. " No improvement! Did you sit up too late last night? Decidedly there is something wrong! You must go out—take rides on horseback. This exercise will be good for you. Buy a little horse; do you hear?"

Gellert smiled. " Buy, always buy! Have you any more prescriptions as economical as this one? They will be just as much to the purpose!"

" And this stove," said the doctor; " it must be heated if the last faggot goes in it. I will give my orders below. Now, my dear professor, God be with you!" Saying these words, he bowed hastily, and went out, before Gillert had time to rise to accompany him to the door.

2

"Kind and skilful man!" said the latter; "but if I followed all his prescriptions, all old Neidhardt's money would scarcely suffice."

The remembrance of this name gave another direction to Gellert's thoughts. The melancholy expression of his face disappeared, and his features betrayed more pleasant emotions. He was so much absorbed, that, having gone to the window, he did not even hear the noise made by the landlady in putting into the stove the wood ordered by the doctor.

Now, we must relate the history of those thirty thalers which Gellert had set apart to replenish his provision of wood. The day before he had made use of them, which, although it showed the goodness of his heart, rendered his enjoyment of a warm stove during that winter extremely uncertain.

FIRST DAY

(17)

FIRST DAY.

In one of the most remote streets of Leipsig, an obscure corner which had escaped the many misfortunes of the city, stood a little house, old and decayed, which belonged to a usurer, as miserly as he was rich, named Neidhardt. Although he was born there, he would have sold it long ago, if he had not calculated that it would be more to his advantage to rent it. He himself occupied a fine house in the market-place.

As he went to no expense either in repairing or keeping this little house in order, it was very much dilapidated. The floors were loose and rotten, the walls damp, and the worm-eaten casements could hardly support the iron frame which held the small dim panes, enclosed in lead. For years it had been rented to a poor shoemaker, whose whole family was larger than his custom, and who, particularly in this time of war and scarcity, with difficulty gained enough, by the sweat of his brow, to pay the rent.

This was a truly honest and God-fearing family. Things went on well enough as long as the father could labor, but, having been very ill the summer before, he could not gain strength enough, on his scanty fare, to go on with his work.

Want had at length entered the poor dwelling, and the children could only bring themselves to beg when forced by the iron hand of poverty. The back-rent now amounted to thirty thalers, and these unhappy people looked forward with dismay to the time when old Neidhardt would use force to make their condition yet more deplorable. The poor wife had begged him, on her knees, to have patience, but he repulsed her harshly, declaring that he would turn them out of doors, if, in one month, they had not paid their debt. And he was a man to execute his menace.

When she related this to her husband, it was such a shock to him that he fell sick again, and from that time grew weaker and weaker Who could tell all the sighs and tears of the mother and children? The dreaded day approached. It was now winter. An icy wind penetrated through the broken window into this damp and gloomy room, the shelter of misery without hope. In one corner, stretched on a truckle-bed, lay the poor father, the signs of death already visible on his pale countenance. Six shivering, hungry little children, cowered, crying, around a fireless stove. What a picture for a mother's heart!

This unhappy woman was there, wringing her hands, but with dry eyes. She had no more tears to shed. Suddenly the sick man turned on his pallet, and said, in a feeble voice, " Though we cannot move the pity of man, the compassion of God is not exhausted; 'Call upon me in the day of trouble,' he says to us; 'I will deliver thee, and thou shalt glorify me!' Come, my dear wife, my dear children, let us pray to the Lord. He will never forsake us."

Encouraged by this promise, the mother and children knelt down by the bed. The sick man sat up—joined his hands—and, raising to heaven his eyes, with an expression of filial assurance, uttered, with fervor, a prayer full of the joy of the Holy Ghost.

When he said Amen, it seemed as if the God of all consolation, who had given them this promise in his Word, himself said yea and amen to their prayer. They arose with new confidence. The mother and the two eldest took up their baskets to go beyond the city to look for chips, which the carpenters who worked there did not hinder the poor from picking up. The younger went out to beg for bread, with the exception of the smallest, who remained with his father. All this passed during the morning of the day on which old Neidhardt had threatened to proceed to extremities.

The sky was clear and cloudless; the air perfectly transparent. The morning sun darted, without obstruction, his rays on the hard-frozen ground, and the easterly wind, which whistled through the streets, penetrated the scanty clothing of these poor famished creatures, as they went to gather those bits which the carpenters thought **not** worth saving.

This same morning Gellert felt himself drawn by an irresistible attraction to go out of the city. Neither the cold that reigned without, nor the mild temperature of his chamber, could withhold him. Wrapping himself in a warm coat, he took his hat and cane, and directed his steps to exactly the same gate whither those poor people were also going.

Meantime the children, benumbed with cold by the icy wind, complained bitterly to their mother.

"Run on fast," said she; "that will warm you." So they ran on with a light step, their mother following at a distance—for care and sorrow are heavy.

3

When she reached the gate of the city, and no longer in sight of her children, all the weight of her misery fell back upon her heart; her tears flowed anew in abundance, and, incapable of standing, she sat down on a stone near the road.

She was still there when Gellert passed that way, and observed this woman weeping aside, her head hidden in her apron, and absorbed in her grief. This sight arrested his steps.

Gellert was familiar with want and distress. At Haynichen, in the house of his father,—who, though a poor pastor with a small salary, saw thirteen children around his table,—these were not infrequent guests, and his own career could attest the difficulties of the poor in conquering the obstacles which they meet in the world. But it is a well-known truth, that the heart of the poor is more compassionate and ready for self-sacrifice than that of the rich; for it seems as if money possessed a petrifying power, which explains, in part, the declaration of our Lord, "It is easier for a camel to go through the eye of a needle, than for a rich man to enter into the kingdom of God." Gellert stood motionless, seeing the woman weep, and many recollections crossed his mind, like the gentle breeze which, caressing the Æolian harp, awakens striking harmonies.

The highway this cold morning was nearly deserted, but the heart of Gellert was crowded with warm emotions;

he felt that he had a good work to do, and that he ought to show himself willing, according to his power.

Softly approaching the woman and putting his hand on her shoulder, he said to her as the Saviour had said before to the widow at the gate of Nain, "Weep not!" The woman, whom grief had rendered unconscious of what passed around her, started at these words, and tremblingly raised her tearful eyes to the man who spoke; but this man seemed so kind, so good, so compassionate! She was reassured; but, notwithstanding, said nothing. Profound misery shuts the heart and the mouth as with a gate of brass. It retires within itself, for it knows that real sympathy is a rare thing, and this experience encases the heart as with a covering of ice, which is hard to melt. As she was still silent, he employed such touching words to gain her confidence, that, involuntarily, the woman lifted her eyes to him a second time. And the gate of brass began to open, and the covering of ice to melt. She felt herself constrained to tell this man, whom she did not know, all that oppressed her. Her tongue was loosed, and she related to him the story of her past and present distress; how the recollection had suddenly overwhelmed her, and how tears had brought some relief; but she added that their worst trouble threatened them that very day. She told him what Neidhardt had resolved, and

3*

which he would not fail to accomplish, as she had not even money enough to buy medicines for her husband and bread for her children, and how much less to pay this debt of thirty thalers! "Ah!" cried she, "my husband will sink under his sickness, and I and my children will die of hunger! Why is it not already over? for there is no hope for us but in the grave!"

"God lives!" said Gellert, in a solemn voice; "the heart of man 'is in the hand of the Lord, as the rivers of water: he turneth it whithersoever he will.'" These words touched the poor woman's heart. She rose, and taking his hand, "Do you believe that He will help us?" said she, in a trembling voice.

"*I believe it*," replied Gellert, with energy ; for the Lord was working in his heart, and he had already come to a determination. He must give all that he had laid by, but he saw only one object—people in despair who must be succored. "Come with me," said he to the woman, "and you shall see that the eternal God always lives to save us from misery and death."

So saying, he took the road to his dwelling. "Oh ! sir," exclaimed the woman, quite comforted, "lét me only go and tell my children !" She ran to the poor little things, who had already filled their baskets ; then returning, followed him, her heart full of hope and thanksgiving.

With joyous feelings he reached

home, opened his desk, and taking out a roll of money, gave it to the woman, saying, "Here are thirty thalers with no curse upon them."

And as the woman, in the excess of her joy and gratitude, attempted to throw herself at his feet, he raised her, saying, "Give thanks to God, who, having heard your prayer, sent me to you. It is He whom you must praise. But," added he, "wait until eleven o'clock before you take this money to old Neidhardt." When the woman had gone, Gellert thanked the Lord on his knees for having condescended to choose him as the instrument of His merciful designs. He supplicated Him to finish His work, and to bless that which he now proposed to attempt.

The hour drew near, and Gellert hastened to Neidhardt's house.

He had never walked through the streets of Leipsig with a lighter heart. He experienced the word of the Lord, " It is more blessed to give than to receive."

Arriving at Neidhardt's, he knocked at the door, and on hearing " Come in " uttered in a peevish and disagreeable voice, he entered the room.

The old usurer, sitting by his table, was piling up little heaps of gold pieces. It could be seen on his face how much Gellert's visit vexed him at this time. Sweeping his money into a drawer, which he shut impatiently, he was going to indulge his visitor with a very unamiable question, when Gellert sa luted him politely, fixing upon him eyes full of openness and honesty, and which now shone with the overflowing happiness which filled his soul.

This look disarmed the old man. Feeling that he owed some respect to one who was the object of general consideration, he offered him a chair, asking to what cause he was indebted for his early visit.

Gellert, happy to see the old man's face more propitious, without waiting to answer his question, came immediately to the point: " I think, Master Neidhardt," said he, " that I must have much to learn from you, for a man so blessed by the Lord cannot fail to make the best use of his riches. You doubtless understand the great art of giving."

Neidhardt, whose thoughts were perhaps still on his money, felt nevertheless the thorny nature of this question,
so frankly asked; and at the bottom of
his heart, a voice which calls things
by their right names, may have said
to him, "Sinful man, is this true?
What canst thou answer?" He changed color a little; the reply which could
only have been a falsehood, trembled
on his tongue, and he could not find
another; at last in his embarrassment
he muttered between his teeth, "Oh,
certainly! h'm, h'm!" or something of
the kind.

Gellert either did not or would not
hear. In short, with that warmth of
feeling which was peculiar to him, he
began to speak of the inexpressible

happiness of doing good. Having just experienced it, his words flowed from the abundance of his heart with such force and, moving eloquence, that the old man, trembling at first, was soon warmed by his animation and awakened to new emotions. Gellert perceived it, and, overcome in turn, he used still more striking appeals, which by the praise of God profoundly affected the old miser. The clock here struck eleven: at that moment a knock was heard, and the poor woman entered, her face beaming with joy. Laying on the table the gift of Gellert, "Here is the money," said she, "but give me back the letter which my husband wrote to you from his sick-bed, to entreat you not to turn us out of doors!"

The old man turned pale, mechanically stretching out his trembling hand. Before Gellert, whose pathetic language had touched him so deeply, the words of this distressed woman were a humiliating sentence, which now came with double weight. Shame, mortification, and repentance, all overwhelmed him together, with a power hitherto unknown. At last, recovering himself a little, he said in a broken voice, "Oh! it was not — so urgent! Why do you talk so? I had not any serious intention—a threat—nothing more! but —go, now; don't you see I have a visitor?"

And clutching the money with his bony fingers, he thrust it into a pocket of his dressing-gown.

4

Gellert who was watching his countenance had not lost a single movement. He said, almost without knowing it, and in a whisper, "Thirty thalers, and with no curse upon them!"

Neidhardt started, and a shiver ran through his frame.

"Yes, yes," continued the woman, "you say now that there was no hurry, because before this charitable man you are ashamed of your hard-heartedness! but yesterday, when I came to implore you to have pity, you drove me away, and said, 'All your tears are of no use! I must have the money, the money, or I will turn you and your rags into the street!' Have you forgotten that? Oh! Master Neidhardt, I did not curse you, but God saw my affliction, and he promises to bless the merciful. To have eaten nothing for twenty-four hours, and be turned into the street with a sick husband, was hard indeed. Our Saviour says, ' With the measure ye mete, it shall be measured unto you!' You can never know what I and mine suffered. When I went home my pious husband prayed with us; he prayed for you, Master Neidhardt, that God would change your heart of stone into a heart of flesh. Then I went out to pick up chips with my children, because during all this cold weather we have been without wood, and when I felt as if I should sink under the weight of our misfortunes, this kind gentleman met me, and gave me those thirty thalers."

All Gellert's signals were useless. "No," she went on, "don't make signs for me to stop; my heart will burst if I cannot speak!"

Neidhardt turned suddenly round, and looked at Gellert with a scrutinizing gaze. The latter was confused, and cast down his eyes.

"Oh! the gentleman is not rich—I saw that very well," continued the woman; "but he is rich in charity! May God's greatest blessings rest upon him!"

"What, was it you," cried the astonished old man; "was it you who did that?" The finger of God had touched him; the blessing pronounced by the woman upon Gellert, transfixed him. The heart of stone gave place to a heart of flesh; going to his bureau, he took from it a paper which he gave to the woman.

"Here," said he, "is your husband's letter, and moreover, the thirty thalers. Take it to buy comforts for him, and bread for your children. Your debt is paid."

And finding in his account-book the register of the debt, he crossed it out with a firm stroke. Then taking Gellert's hand, with emotion, "Excellent man," said he, "your words are beautiful and good, but your actions are noble! May God reward you! But to repair in some measure the wrongs which I have done, suffer me to accompany you to the dwelling of this poor family. I will try to show myself under a more favorable aspect."

4*

The woman stood like a statue.

When she came to herself, tears fell from her eyes.

"Oh! I see now," cried she, "that 'the prayer of a righteous man availeth much!' Oh! Master Neidhardt, pardon me my evil thoughts of you. May God bless you! And you," said she to Gellert, "you are our good angel; how can we thank you enough?"

They went out, and soon came to the ruined house, and to that chamber which had been the hiding-place of so many griefs. But the mother's story came like a beam of sunshine after a dark day. The father and children stretched their hands eagerly to their benefactors, and the expressions of their gratitude were inexhaustible. "The

Lord has heard our prayers, dear wife. His Name be praised," cried the sick man.

Old Neidhardt wept with joy, so much was he overcome by the thanks of these good people. Gellert spoke some comforting words to the invalid, which gave him fresh heart. He promised to send him his friend, the physician, and Neidhardt confirmed this promise.

And, besides, this was not the limit of the old man's benefits. He apprenticed the shoemaker's son to a tradesman, paying the fees for him, as well as the schooling of the other children. He gave clothes to all, and allowed them their house rent free. We will here anticipate and say, that the shoemaker recovered; and, with Neidhardt's assistance, his trade soon became prosperous.

From this time forward, the old man seemed to be transformed, and remained until his death a most devoted friend and admirer of Gellert. It was in this way that Gellert had deprived himself of his thirty thalers. And though he was thus impoverished, he was by so much richer in heart; and in his secret place of prayer he thanked him who had thus blessed his words and works.

SECOND DAY.

SECOND DAY.

In going out of Gellert's room, the doctor met the housemaid.

"Show me the professor's firewood," said he.

She took him to the wood-shed. "This is not very encouraging," she remarked, "if some more does not come in soon."

"No matter," said the doctor, shaking his head, "his chamber must be heated! Do it as it ought to be done!" And he went out precipitately, being in haste to read Gellert's hymn to his wife. But he was not to have this pleasure to-day. He had hardly reach-ed the street which led to his house, when a poor woman accosted him.

"Oh! dear sir," cried she, "come, I pray you, to see my husband, of whom the Professor Gellert must have told you. And old Neidhardt, too, wished me to go for you. He is very ill."

"My good Gellert," said the doctor to himself; "and how do you know him?" he asked the woman.

Gratitude is communicative, she be-gan her story—"Come, come," inter-rupted the doctor, "tell me as we walk along." Nevertheless, he stopped more than once in the lonely street better to understand this story, which so deeply touched his excellent heart.

"Oh! I know now where his money

went to, and why he is as poor as a church mouse! I understand why his room is cold, and why he can buy no wood! Generous man! May God restore it to thee!"

It was only then that the woman understood the greatness of the sacrifice which Gellert had made for her.

But as she expressed her sorrow, "No matter," said the doctor, "he will certainly have some more money, and some more wood. Believe me, God does not desert such men."

When they reached the house, the doctor gave the necessary prescriptions; then quickly retraced his steps, his head and heart full of Gellert's kind deed, and of the disastrous consequences it might bring upon him.

5

Approaching his own door, he saw before it a fine horse already saddled, which a countryman held by the bridle.

"What do you want?" he asked the man.

"The burgomaster of ——," and he named a village in the environs of Leipsig, " begs you, for God's sake, to come as quickly as possible—it is for our lady, who is in painful labor. Oh! sir, our good master will be in despair if you do not hurry. She is very ill."

The doctor was not only a skilful and enthusiastic physician, but had, besides, a sensitive and sympathizing heart.

" My wife will have to wait for the hymn," thought he. He sprang up the steps two at a time, got his instruments, kissed his wife, ran down again, threw himself into the saddle, and set off, followed by the servant.

The road was obstructed by artillery, and all sorts of Prussian troops. It was difficult to force a way through, still the doctor arrived in good time. He got off before a large farm-house, which the man pointed out as belonging to his master. A person came out, with an anxious and distressed countenance. After a few words exchanged in a low voice, the doctor followed him up stairs. At the end of an hour they came down. The features of the doctor expressed satisfaction, and, on the face of the burgomaster, anguish was exchanged for joy.

They entered together the great hall,

where a large number of superior officers were sitting down to dinner.

The doctor was invited to take a
place at table, and the burgomaster,
who was also an inn-keeper, directed
the service.

Among these officers there was one
whom the others treated with the greatest respect, though nothing distinguished him from the rest, if it were not for
an air of dignity, tempered by an expression of mildness and benevolence.

The doctor had earned a good appe-
tite, and without heeding the conversation of the officers, worked valiantly to
satisfy it, his host doing his best for
him, and continually handing him new
dishes.

" You are from Leipsig, doctor," said

the distinguished personage, who had heard the burgomaster give him this title.

"At your service," said the doctor, without ceasing from his employment, which he pursued with as much ardor as success.

"Then you probably know the Professor Gellert?" again asked the same voice.

This time the doctor put down his fork to look at his questioner; the impression which he had made being favorable, he answered, "I am his physician, and I may add with pride, his friend!"

"Ah! indeed," said the unknown; "I have heard that he is an invalid?"

"Alas, yes. That which he needs

in common with most literary men is exercise. The best thing for him would be to ride on horse-back. So I told him he ought to buy a nice pony."

"And does he mean to?"

"His will is good, but the power is wanting." And here the doctor, pressing his thumb and fore finger together, made an expressive sign.

"What! is he so poor?" asked the unknown, with interest.

"As a church mouse," quickly replied the doctor. "If you will allow me, I will tell you how I found him this morning."

And upon the unknown expressing a warm desire to hear it, the impulsive doctor related from beginning to end, with scrupulous exactness, that which we have sketched in the two previous chapters. When he had finished, his interrogator, quite overcome, said, clasping his hands, "Such a generous man, to suffer from want, and go without a horse because he gives his last dollar to the poor!"

The doctor was in a communicative vein. "Since you are so much interested in our noble poet," said he, taking a paper from his pocket, "you will like, perhaps, to read the hymn which he had just composed this morning, under the influence of the scriptural thoughts which filled his mind?" and handing the sheet to the officer, he added, "It is the original manuscript; I asked him for it in order to take a copy, which the duties of my profession have until now hindered me from doing."

The officer took the paper eagerly. Then he said, " A new hymn by the poet whom we all so justly honor, should belong to all. I will read it aloud." He then read, with much expression and feeling, the following hymn :

" What! shall we receive good at the hand of God, and shall we not receive evil ? "—Job ii. 20.

" I have had my days of blessing,*
    All the joys of life possessing,
        Unnumber'd they appear !
    Then let faith and patience cheer me,
    Now that trials gather near me ;
        Where is life without a tear ?

" Yes, O Lord! a sinner looking
    O'er the sins Thou art rebuking,

* We have taken this translation from the " Hymns from the Land of Luther."

Must own Thy judgments light.
Surely I, so oft offending,
Must, in humble patience bending,
    Feel Thy chastisements are right.

" Let me, o'er transgression weeping,
    Find the grace my soul is seeking;
        Receiving at Thy throne
Strength to meet each tribulation,
Looking for the great salvation,
    Trusting in my Lord alone.

" While, 'mid earthly tears and sighing,
    Still to praise Thee, feebly trying,
        Still clinging, Lord, to Thee:
Quietly on Thy love relying,
I am Thine—and, living, dying,
    Surely all is well with me."

The guests were silent long after the reading had ceased.

The impression was deep and general. The burgomaster in particular was much overcome, for God had just granted him a great deliverance.

"Doctor," at length said the un-known, "may I venture to beg your permission to copy this hymn? at least, if you have leisure to wait a few mo-ments?"

"There is nothing to prevent, it ap-pears to me."

"My dear Noslits," said the un-known to our military officer, "take this, I pray, and copy it quickly." The officer thus summoned took the paper eagerly, and went out.

"And you say," cried the burgomas-ter, "that the author of this hymn, so full of sincere faith, and of so many other beautiful hymns, has nothing to warm him, though he is sick, in this severe weather?"

"Nothing can be more true," replied

the doctor. "I found him this morning in a cold room."

"Ah! sooner than that should be so, I would rather tremble with cold like a greyhound, for a week, and —" here a general burst of laughter greeted these words of the burgomaster, notwithstanding the serious impression which Gellert's hymn had made on all the company.

The good man thought that these gentlemen doubted his performance of the resolution which he had made internally, but which he had not yet expressed. Putting his hand on his breast, he said, with an injured voice, "Yes, as truly as I have just been delivered from a great affliction, I will send to him this very day such a load of wood as has never yet rolled over the streets of Leipsig!"

And calling from the window to his man,—" Peter," said he, " take the large cart which we send to market, load it with as much wood as it will carry, harness four horses, and go into Leipsig.   Inquire for the house of Professor Gellert, unload the wood before his door, present my compliments, and tell him that it is a present for the beautiful hymn, 'I have had my days of blessing;' but above all, go quickly. He must have it to-day."

" Yes, sir, it shall be done," said the servant, going away.

" Bravo!" cried all the officers in chorus, " bravo ! burgomaster."

" You are a man of honor," said the

unknown; "you have just set me an example which I shall remember."

The conversation still ran upon Gellert; the doctor had many questions to answer about his life, his habits, etc., which he did willingly, for he loved Gellert with a warm and devoted affection.

At last the artillery officer came back with the copy, which he gave to his superior, and the latter with many thanks returned the original to the doctor.

But the burgomaster, taking it out of his hands, "Doctor," cried he, "allow me to take a copy in my turn?"

"Very willingly, if you will give it to me before I depart."

"Certainly; but as I have not time

6

to copy it myself, I will send to our chorister, who is a good writer and has a steady hand."

Which he did accordingly, and the doctor, having taken leave of the company, went out to see his patient.

Seeing before the door a groom holding a magnificent horse, he asked him who that officer was to whom the others showed so much respect. "It is the Prince of Prussia, worthy sir," replied the groom.

The doctor, striking his forehead, rushed up stairs.

A little while after, a clattering of hoofs and the gallop of horses resounded in the air. It was the prince and his suite riding towards Leipsig.

Then the cracking of a whip was

heard. The burgomaster drew the doctor towards a window which looked out on the court. Four large draught-horses started out without difficulty an enormous cart loaded with beech wood.

"Have I kept my word?" said the burgomaster.

"Capitally!" cried the doctor. "I would only like to see the surprise with which that will be received. May God reward you!"

The mother and child being as well as could be desired, the doctor was soon able to think of returning, which was all the more agreeable to him, as, many troops having entered Leipsig, it was to be feared they would take up their quarters there.

Having at last obtained possession

of his manuscript, he left the village; and on his return to the city he could, without interruption, enjoy the pleasure of his wife on reading the hymn, as well as her wonder at the remarkable results of the last two days.

At the same time that the doctor, without being aware of it, was seated at table with the excellent Prince Henry of Prussia, Gellert went out, according to his prescription, to take some exercise, and directed his steps towards the same place where he had met the poor woman. All the occurrences of the day before were present to his mind as distinctly as if they had taken place a second time; but the thought of his thirty thalers did not even cause a sigh; though, if a beggar had accosted him now, he could not have bestowed even the smallest alms.

In his preoccupation he extended his walk further than usual, and it was almost evening when he reached his dwelling.

What was his astonishment when he saw before the door a quantity of fire-wood, over which three wood-cutters were hard at work, without any prospect of finishing that day, the pile was so large! He said to himself, with a slight smile, that he would be very happy to have one like it. When he came up to the men they saluted him with respect, as he was well-known in

Leipsig. "Sir," said one of them, "you have bought a load of wood as large as two common ones. We can hardly finish it to-morrow. And it is as hard as iron, too.

"I! bought wood!" said Gellert, thinking of his empty purse; "what do you say? You have made a mistake, my good men!" He went in without stopping. The wood-cutters looked at each other, and laughed. "There goes one of our wise men, who would leave their heads somewhere about if they were not well planted on their shoulders," said one of them.

"Peace," cried another. "Leipsig has reason to be proud of that man. It is he who writes so many beautiful hymns."

During this little altercation, Gellert met his landlady.

"I congratulate you, Professor," said she, with a smiling face.

"And for what?" said the astonished Gellert.

"Well, you had hardly gone out, when a load of wood, drawn by four horses, stopped before the door. 'Who is it for?' said I. 'Eh,' said the driver, 'I am the servant of the burgomaster of ——, and I have brought this wood to Professor Gellert. Does he not live here?' 'Certainly,' said I, 'he lives with us, but he has gone out.' 'No matter,' replied he, 'I will unload all the same, and give my message to you, and you can tell him.' And he unloaded and unloaded, till I thought it would never stop. A real mountain, I tell you. So I had to send for the wood-cutters, for fear of the police. See, they have worked several hours, and the pile is no smaller. Now they will have to put it in the yard, for it must not be left in the street. I know it by experience, for I can tell you a story about the police, who don't trifle in Leipsig."

"Excuse me," interrupted Gellert, who knew that, once set going with her anecdotes, the good woman had enough to last an age; "but tell me how much this wood costs, and then"—

"What it costs? Sir, it costs nothing, absolutely nothing, for it's a present."

"What do you mean?" cried Gellert, more and more surprised.

" Certainly it is, and here is the message, word for word :" and she repeated, with scrupulous exactness, all that the servant had said in his master's name.

Gellert could not contain his surprise. "It is for the hymn, 'I have had my days of blessing,' repeated he, after a pause; did he say it in those very words?"

" In those very words. It must be a new hymn, for I have not seen it."

Gellert shook his head doubtfully, for he saw no connection between these things. He understood still less by what means the hymn had come to the knowledge of the burgomaster in such a short time, and under such unfavorable circumstances. But the facts spoke louder than any reasoning. The wood was there—cost nothing—would last all winter, and was of the best quality. If there were not behind it some mistake, which would have to be paid for afterwards, it was —— a miracle.

Nevertheless, by dint of hearing the landlady relate all the circumstances in detail, and report the expressions of the message, he would no longer disbelieve it.

Gellert went up to his study, which he found delightfully warm, and, putting on his dressing-gown, sat down in the old arm-chair in which his father at Haynichen had passed so many troubled hours. But Gellert was much more cheerful than when he sat there in the morning. Had not God sent him this favor at the very time when he most needed it? He thanked him with all his heart; ate the soup, which they brought him, as usual; studied for some time afterwards, and then went to bed, promising himself that, when the road was no longer encumbered by troops, he would go to the burgomaster of ——, and ask him to explain this mystery. He did not think of the doctor. What had he to do with the burgomaster of ——, and, above all, when the troops came from that direction? While he was quietly going to sleep, the absence of any connection between all these circumstances caused him once more to shake his head.

THIRD DAY.

THIRD DAY

The next morning the doctor did not fail to think of Gellert, and intended to go and explain to him the mystery of the wood. But he was again to be denied this pleasure. He received at an early hour many billets for quartering the soldiers, and he had hardly time to visit his patients. In his rapid course through the streets he heard his name called from a window, and, raising his eyes, saw old Neidhardt making signs in the most earnest manner for him to come to him. "How is the shoemaker?" said he, after a short greeting.

"Ah!" said the doctor, " you gave him a more effectual remedy than any of my prescriptions."

" Doctor," said the old man, much moved, " It is your excellent friend, the worthy professor Gellert, who has done all. If it were not for him I should still be going in my old ways, which I now condemn."

" Very well, only follow the same treatment with our poor man, and I will answer for it that in a week he will be as hardy as an oak. But, by the way, Master Neidhardt, do you understand this matter in all its details? Do you know the sacrifice which Gellert made in giving away those thirty thalers?"

" And how?"

"Well, you must know that Gellert is very poor. The thirty thalers which he gave to the poor shoemaker's wife were all that he had laid up, and since the day before yesterday he has been entirely bare, and does not know where to find a penny. Nevertheless he gave away all, without thinking of himself, solely occupied with the sufferings of these poor people."

Neidhardt's heart was really changed.

"Can it be true?" cried he, clasping his hands.

"As true as the December sun shines into this room," answered the doctor. "But I must read you the verses which he composed under these circumstances." And he read the

7*

hymn which he carried about, always intending to return it to Gellert.

The old man listened with true appreciation. "It is admirable," cried he. "What a man this Gellert is! Allow me, docter, to copy it?"

"I would consent with all my heart, were I not obliged to take it back to him."

"But are you not going to see the poor shoemaker? On your return you can stop for it."

"Very well," said the doctor, hurrying off.

The old man quickly copied the hymn. Then he read it over and over again. "What!" said he, "shall such a man be in distress, while I have enough and to spare? He has shown me the right way, and since then I know the joy of doing good. I will send back to him these thirty thalers. He must have them without knowing from whence they came. He hastened to his secretary, took from thence a roll of thirty thalers, wrote on it, "For the beautiful hymn, 'I have had my days of blessing,' etc.," and gave it to his errand-boy with orders to deliver it to Gellert in person, and come away immediately; on no account to tell him who sent it.

Gellert was seated by his table, absorbed in study. A knock was heard and a servant entered, placed a roll of money on the table, and disappeared like lightning.

Gellert in amazement took the roll,

read the superscription, and let it fall on the table.

"Explain this who can!" cried he. "Can this hymn then be printed and published? It is impossible! Perhaps the doctor—but no! He knows nothing of this poor family, and I have not even been able to send him there yet. God alone knows the connection between all these things."

But as he racked his brains, a knock was again heard at the door.

This time the visitor was a staff-officer of the Prussian army. "Have I the honor of speaking to Professor Gellert?" said he, on entering.

"At your service," answered the latter, with great respect.

"His Royal Highness Prince Henry

of Prussia, who has been here since yesterday, wishes to speak with you, sir; and he asks, since you are an invalid, when he may come to pay his respects?"

"His respects! to me? A prince royal of Prussia pay his respects to me? There must be some misunderstanding or some mistake in the message. Have the goodness, I pray you, to inform his Royal Highness that I shall be extremely honored in paying him my very humble duty, if it will please him to appoint the time; and all the more that I am not confined to my bed, as you see."

The adjutant was amused by the consternation of the man of letters, whom the prince's condescension seemed to put quite out of countenance. "Do not let that trouble you, Professor," said he; "His Royal Highness really did use that expression, which only shows the high regard he has for your person. But if you will give him the pleasure of a visit, allow me the honor of conducting you, if it is agreeable."

"Then have the goodness to allow me to dress," said Gellert.

The adjutant bowed, and Gellert, going into his bed-chamber, was not slow in reappearing in his best clothes, all ready to accompany him. As they entered the presence of the prince the latter hastened to Gellert, gave him his hand, and loaded him with expressions of kindness. "I am particularly delighted," said he "to see before me the author of the beautiful hymn, 'I have had my days of blessing.'"

We may imagine Gellert's embarrassment in hearing the prince also speak of this hymn. He no longer doubted that it had been given to the public, however inexplicable the thing might be. He could hardly contain his desire of asking the prince how he came to know this hymn. But he said nothing, not thinking it proper or respectful to ask such a question. "They told me," resumed the prince, "that you were an invalid. I rejoice to find you better than I had expected. Your appearance, nevertheless, does not indicate good health, and I suppose we must conclude that you do not take enough exercise."

"My calling obliges me to study," said Gellert, bowing.

"Without doubt," continued the prince, "but you must think of preserving for the German people their favorite poet, and take more care of yourself."

"Your Royal Highness may rest assured that I do all I can."

"Yes, but that is not enough. How often the bad walking must keep you at home, without speaking of other hindrances! You should take a ride on horseback every day. No other exercise is so good for those whose calling or duties oblige them to sit habitually."

"Your Royal Highness is right— my physician gives me the same advice; but every one has not the means——"

"Yes," interrupted the prince, "no one can have the means, who has also a heart so charitable as to give, at once, to a needy family, his last thirty thalers!"

Gellert would have liked to be a hundred feet under ground. Everything was then known: his head swam.

The prince saw his embarrassment, and taking his hand, exclaimed, "Generous man, I know your way of doing things, and I am far from being inclined to blame in you that which can only come from the riches of the grace of God. Yes, may He reward you; but permit me to offer you from my stable a little horse, whose gentleness renders him fit for the service of a man of peace."

"Your Royal Highness—" stammered the poet—but he could go no further; emotion and surprise prevented him from saying another word.

The prince, himself overcome, pressed his hand; then, wishing to put an end to his thanks, he said, "Other duties call me. Farewell! May heaven long preserve to us such a precious life, and may the little horse do his part;" and bowing, he retired to the next room.

Gellert remained for some time absent and motionless. The adjutant approached him.

"You see, Professor, that a prince

will not be behind a village burgomaster."

Gellert looked at him fixedly.

"And how did his royal highness
know all that?" stammered he.

The adjutant smiled.

"Princes," said he, "are doubtless
ignorant of many things, but they often
know more than other mortals. Do
not disturb yourself about it, but make
frequent use of the prince's present."

Gellert understood that it was time
to retire, but he did not do so until he
had begged the adjutant to testify his
profound gratitude to the prince. The
adjutant reconducted him to the door.

Enigmas had followed enigmas, and
for three days it had seemed as if every
thing happened to him by some magic

power. At times he thought he **was** dreaming; but on reaching home he saw the wood-cutters still busy, and before the door one of the prince's grooms, with a beautiful horse, perfectly equipped, which he presented from his master.

"It is the time of signs and miracles, Professor," cried the landlady. "Yesterday this magnificent pile of wood; to-day a splendid horse! When will it end?"

"Do not be anxious," said Gellert, smiling; "everything has its limits."

Towards the evening of the same day, Gellert was seated in his study; he had paid the wood-cutters, and there still remained a great deal of money. He possessed a fine horse. The most

lively gratitude to God filled his soul.
He took his pen and wrote another
beautiful hymn :

I.

How great the goodness of the Lord!
Can any man so dull, be found,
Whose hardened soul will not be moved
His love to feel—His praise to sound?
No! be it still my highest aim
To measure His almighty love!
My God has not forgotten me,
My heart shall not ungrateful prove.

II.

Who, but this God who needs me not,
First formed me by His wondrous power?
And though His counsel I reject,
He leads me on, from hour to hour.
Who gives my conscience inward peace?
Who lifts my soul when it would fall?
Who gives me much that's good to enjoy?
His gracious hand provides it all.

III.

Then, O my soul! look at this world
Where He has given thee a place;

8*

The glory that surrounds thee here
 Is but the shadow of His face.
To all these joys thou hast a right,
 Through God's good-will they all are thine;
For thee did Christ endure the cross,
 That thou might'st in His kingdom shine.

IV.

And shall I cease to praise my God,
 Refuse His way to understand?
And shall He call and I not hear,
 Nor see the guiding of His hand?
His will is written on my heart,
 And strength is given by His word:
Him will I love with love supreme,
 And all His children in their Lord.

V.

So shall I best resemble Him,
 If this, my gratitude and love,
Shall stamp His image on my heart,
 And thus my prompt obedience prove.
So shall His love possess my soul,
 Urge it to keep the path that's right;
And though through weakness I may fall,
 Sin shall not triumph in the fight.

VI.

Oh! may Thy goodness and Thy love
　Always remain before my eyes;
And give me needful strength to yield
　My soul a living sacrifice!
In times of joy, may it restrain,
　And comfort me when grief is near;
And so possess my sinking heart,
　That the last foe shall cause no fear!

When he had thus poured out the feelings of his heart, and finished the hymn, the doctor entered.

"Already another hymn!" said he, leaning on the table, upon which he laid the manuscript he had kept so long.

"Yes, but you shall not have this one," said Gellert, "for who knows what you have been doing with the other!" and the good doctor was quite overcome by the story of all that had happened by reason of the hymn.

" Now," said Gellert, " confess what is the meaning of all this."

The doctor looked at him long, with eyes expressive of true happiness.

" I have done nothing," answered he. " It pleased God to cause a special blessing to rest on your hymn; that is all. My worthy friend, I can make costly prescriptions, which I know it is neither in my power nor in that of the apothecary to make up. This time God himself has undertaken them, and that without my knowledge. To Him alone be the glory !" Saying these words, he departed.

" Blind, indeed," says Von Harns, a biographer of Gellert, "must be the soul who would not see in this the finger of God—insensible the heart who would not cry, ' Blessed be the name of the Lord, from this time forth and forever more !' Amen !"

" Be glad in the Lord, and rejoice, ye righteous: and shout for joy, all ye that are upright in heart."

" Verily I say unto you, Inasmuch as ye have done it unto one of the least of these my brethren, ye have done it unto me."

" Call upon me in the day of trouble; I will deliver thee, and thou shalt glorify me."

" For all the promises of God in him are yea, and in him amen."

www.ingramcontent.com/pod-product-compliance
Lightning Source LLC
Chambersburg PA
CBHW020036030726
47499CB00007B/2447